He can get you in a firefighter's carry
before you can say

Uncle Ted put me down!

He says
he's had plenty
of close shaves,
which is funny
because he has a beard.
Mom says Uncle Ted
and I get along
like a house on fire.

This book is for my
sister Rachel, who was
crazy about guinea pigs,
and for my sister Jenny,
who preferred cars.

RACHEL

JENNY

Also for
my friend
Lindsay
Isobel
Hart.

Thanks
to Olga
at the
guinea
pig
rescue
center.

Copyright © 2000 by Lauren Child

All rights reserved.

First U.S. edition 2001

Library of Congress
Cataloging-in-Publication Data
is available.

Library of Congress
Catalog Card Number
00-037963

First published in Great Britain in 2000
by Orchard Books, London.

Designed by
Anna-Louise Billson

ISBN 0-7636-1373-8

2 4 6 8 10 9 7 5 3 1

Printed in Singapore

Candlewick Press
2067 Massachusetts Avenue
Cambridge, Massachusetts 02140

Clarice Bean

Guess Who's Babysitting?

CANDLEWICK PRESS
CAMBRIDGE, MASSACHUSETTS

We got a phone call
at five-fifteen
in the morning.

It turned out Mom's older brother,
Uncle Ernie, *slipped* on a doughnut
getting out of his squad car.

He's a
policeman in
New York City
so he's used
to life's
ups and *downs*.

The
nurse says
could

Mom get out there on the double because he's lying flat on his back with both legs in the air.

Mom says,

What's he doing eating doughnuts at this hour of the day?

But of course she has to go.

Someone will have to babysit because
Dad is also going away, on Important Business.

Marcie (my big sister) says,
**I would rather look after newts
from Neptune than
be left with Clarice Bean** (me)
and Minal Cricket
(my little brother).

Kurt
(my big brother)
says,

Don't look at me, I'm going
to my room and probably
won't be down for supper.

Minal says,
What
about
Grandad?

Grandad says,
I haven't had
a doughnut
since I was
a boy.

Mom phones all her friends for a babysitter. Then she phones all her friends' friends but everybody says they are busy.

Dad says,

Who can **blame** them?

I'll be with you in two shakes, Bernard.

I say,

How about Uncle Ted?

Mom goes a little pale.

Uncle Ted is Mom's younger brother.

When Uncle Ted needs a break from firefighting
and cats up trees he comes over to our house.
And then
things get a little wild.

Get off your horse
and drink your milk.

Uncle Ted and I love to watch Westerns on the edge of our seats
with plates of eggs and beans
perched on our laps.

Uncle Ted is teaching me cowboy techniques.
One time he lassoed the lamp.

Mom said,
*I'd rather have everything in one piece
thank you very much.*

Uncle Ted looked sheepish.
I lassoed my brother.
He wasn't too happy either.

So you can see why Mom is nervous about leaving Uncle Ted in charge but it turns out she can't be so choosy. Mom gives Uncle Ted very **strict** instructions.

1. NO BREAKAGES

2. NO LASSOING

3. DON'T DRIVE MRS. STAMPNEY AT NUMBER 9 WACKO

4. MAKE SURE KURT SEES DAYLIGHT AT LEAST ONCE EVERY 24 HOURS

6. KEEP AN EYE ON GRANDAD HE TENDS TO W A N D E R O F F

5. DON'T LET MARCIE TAKE THE PHONE INTO HER BEDROOM

chat chat chat
chat chat
chat chat
chat
chat
chat

Uncle Ted says,

**Yes, Ma'am.
I hear you
loud and clear.**

Everything goes
really well
for the first two days.

Nobody is arguing
and we are like
one of those families
on television
who always say
things like

please

and

thank you

and

sorry . . .

...and they let people share their stuff without grumbling.

Kurt even sits in the backyard and almost gets a tan. He never normally goes outside. He says it's too bright.

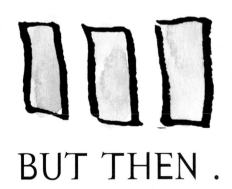

BUT THEN . . .

. . . Minal ruins everything
by taking Albert out of his hutch without asking.

I am supposed to be taking care of him over spring break.
(Albert is the school guinea pig so it's a VERY
RESPONSIBLE
JOB.)

Albert

Albert makes

I am beside myself because I **know** he will never be seen again. Minal and I are racing around the kitchen table. Minal is squealing and I am trying to flick his nose with a carrot.

a run for it.

Lots
of
things
get
broken.

**Drop the
carrot,
little lady.**

Luckily for Minal Cricket,
Uncle Ted comes in to rescue him.

To take my mind off
the worry of
losing a guinea pig
we all go outside
and play soccer.

And it works because Uncle Ted kicks the ball so hard that it knocks Minal out.

We have to **drive** to the e m e r g e n c y r o o m at **50** miles an hour at least!

Hang on to your hats!

Minal is fine
but they still give him an X-ray
and a little carton of orange juice.

Minal loves it
because he can
show off and lie
under a blanket
and whimper.

I say he should
have stitches but
unfortunately the
nurse doesn't agree.

When we get home we find Grandad is missing.
Uncle Ted phones all the neighbors
and is about to dial 911 when
Mrs. Stampney
calls to say she has found Grandad
in
her
living room.

Watching the races.

She's pretty grumpy about it.

Uncle Ted says,

How on earth did you end up here?

Grandad says,
   All the houses look the same
when you get to my **age**.

      But I know it's really because
   Mrs. Stampney has a bigger TV than we do,
         plus, she's got a remote control.

I'm still worried sick about Albert so I go into the yard
to see if he's back in his hutch.

I had left a carrot there
to lure him
but
it's still unnibbled.

The next thing I know,
Robert Granger,
the boy next door,

pops over

the wall.

He says,
Do you want to pet **my guinea pig?**

I say, That's not
your
guinea pig. That's Albert.

He says,
It's not Albert.
It's Belinda.

I say,
You better give him back,
Robert Granger.
That's school property
and you will be
in
big trouble
with the police.

Robert Granger is so nervous
he lets Albert
w r i g g l e
out of his hands.

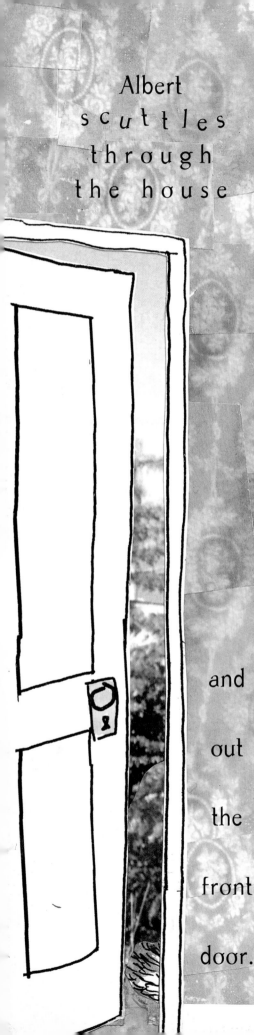

Albert scuttles through the house

and out the front door.

Uncle Ted shouts, **After him!**

We are madly chasing the guinea pig who charges through the fence.

Minal squeezes after him and gets stuck like a giant squeaking tomato. I say, Lucky you are here, Uncle Ted, because you can rescue him in next to no time.

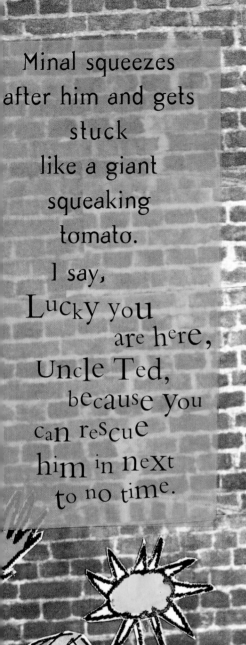

(Rescuing people from fences is normal for Uncle Ted and he doesn't look a bit worried.)

Uncle Ted says, **Hang in there, Buddy.**

He races off to call his friends at the fire station. But it takes him forever to find the phone.

chat
chat
chat
chat
. . . so anyway, I said . . .
chat   chat
. . . and then guess   chat
what he said . . .

chat

chat
chat
chat

In the meantime
Mom comes back from the airport.
She reaches right into her bag
for her new bottle of bubble bath
and rubs it on Minal's head.
She wriggles him free in
two minutes
flat.

Bubble Bath

Then she says,
I think I'd like
a nice relaxing
cup of tea in the backyard.

Guess
what ?

The whole fire
department shows up.
Mom doesn't
look at all
surprised.
She just glares at
Uncle Ted.

Minal is
already rescued.

It turns out Uncle Ernie is feeling much better, but he doesn't think he will ever be able to look at a doughnut again.

He says,
Make mine a
double
cheeseburger
with fries and a
banana
milkshake to go.